# Zombies from Space and Vampires

# Zombies from Space and Vampires

Angela B. Chrysler

Published 2021 by Next Chapter
Cover art by Deranged Doctor Designs

# Acknowledgements

*Here it is again: another acknowledgements page that no one enjoys reading except those who are mentioned in it. Instead, I will take this moment to explain a bit about the characters in Zombies from Space.*

This is a work of fiction, unfortunately. Businesses and places are either the products of the author's imagination or used in a fictitious manner. Events and incidents are formed in the deranged brain of the author, who is still sitting around immersed in an arsenal disguised as a peaceful garden waiting for the zombie apocalypse to occur alongside an alien invasion. The vampires I threw in for fun because... how else do you make a bad story worse?

Names and characters in this book are real people who live vicariously through this story. Any resemblance to actual persons, living or dead, was *completely and totally intentional... and with the exclusive permission of the characters mentioned. All characteristics of said people were also based on their own design.*

*Stanislava D. Kohut named herself Stanushka and asked for pink bubblegum and pink pigtails while she handled her giant bazooka alongside her weapon fetishes. I said, "Okay!"*

*Adam Dreece said, "I want a vest with pockets! Many pockets! And filled with all sorts of trinkets and things! And remember my monocle!" I said, "Okay!"*

*Matthew William Harrill said, "I want to be naked wearing only a garlic-infused loincloth and boots!" I said, "O—okaaaay. . . ?" and added the Doctor Who scarf in ode to Tom Baker and Matt's English heritage. It only felt appropriate to have Matt steal my collector's edition scarf and wrap himself up in it as clothing.*

*His response when reading that? "I would so DO that!" Yes, Matt. . . Yes, you would. And I would so hunt you down for it.*

*Additional characters who deserve mention and recognition are:*

*C.L. Schneider (Cin Dixon)*

*Stan Sudan (The Professor)*

*Kylie "Kraken" Jude*

*Chess DeSalls (Chess "Cutlass" DeSalls)*

*Jay Norry*

*J.S. Swiger*

*M.L.S. Weech, who asked to be one of the zombies. So I gave him honors and made him all of them.*

*And our beloved ship, the HMS Slush Brain! Which is a real discussion group on Twitter we fondly deemed the HMS Slush Brain. No, you can't join. It's a private group for our collective. We hold secret meetings and make plans to take over the world. But due to the slush brain we all possess, I doubt any of us will actually succeed at this. For the record, Matt is our "Pinky." The rest of us are the Brain.*

*Additional characters in this story are all based on real life friends who I portray best to their character and requests (I hope).*

For my fellow nerds.
Game on.

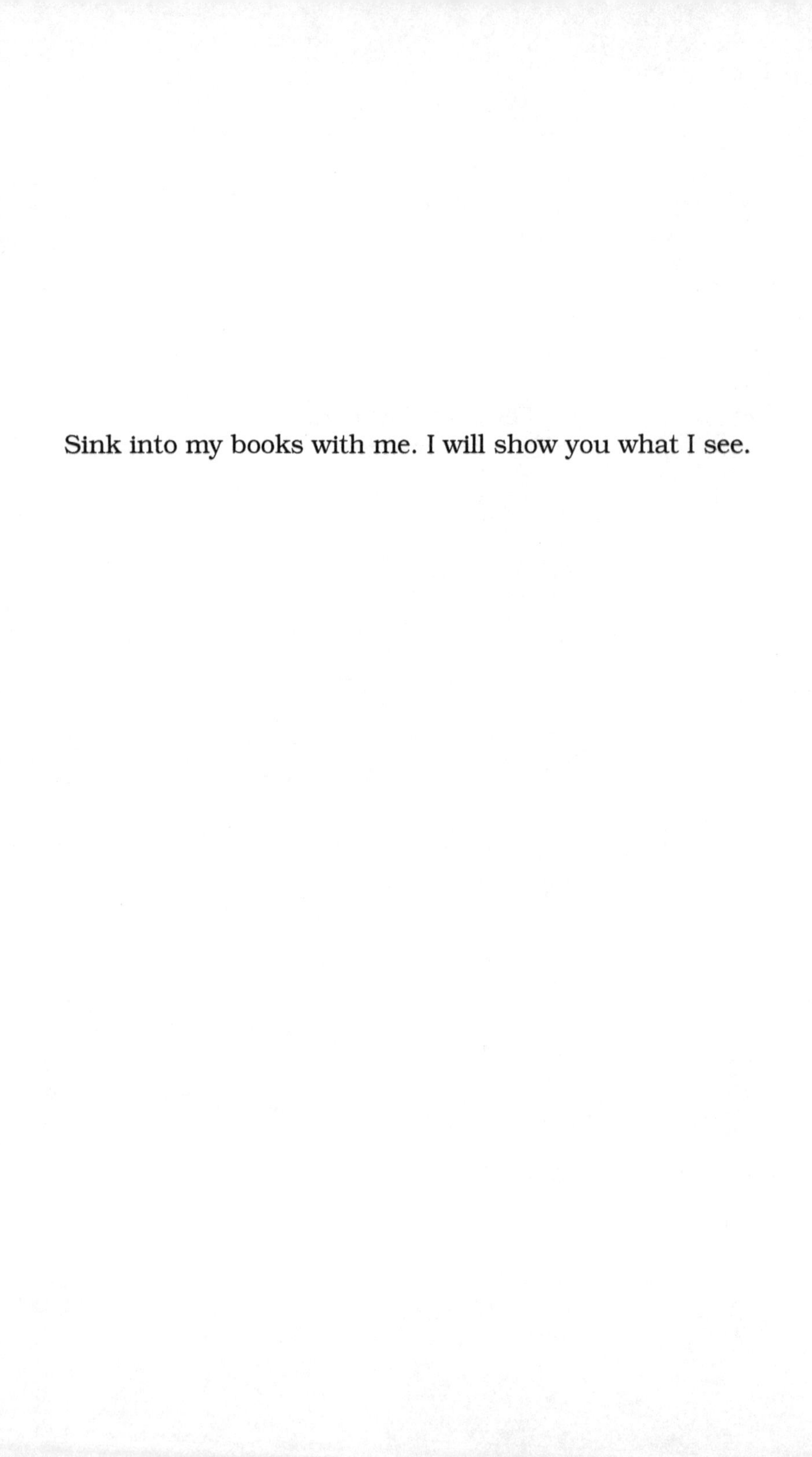

Sink into my books with me. I will show you what I see.

# Introduction

I conceived this idea shortly after watching *Kung Fu Panda 3*. The preview in the beginning showed two guys standing there... "zombies... in space!" After scribbling "zombies from space" on a popcorn napkin, I sat on my idea for the next two hours while I tried not to explode with enthusiasm. (The movie was great, by the way.)

By the time I got home, I had a plot, but I had a challenge presented to me.

My husband is a scientist. More specifically, he is a physicist and holds a master's in organic chemistry. You know that stuff Sheldon Cooper does? That's my husband. My husband is also a heavy sci-fi reader where one rule is gold: "Scientific accuracy." He doesn't watch *The Walking Dead,* so every Monday night, I fill him in on the next episode. His reason for not watching TWD?

"There are too many plot holes based on one ludicrous concept: Zombies are illogical!" he argues.

"Who cares!" I argue back. "They're zombies! They are no more logical than Bruce Campbell and his army of dead."

"Yeah, but... it's Bruce!"

This is where I sigh and call him a zombie-ist.

"Bruce is so damn hokey that he's awesome!" my husband says.

"So you're saying that *Walking Dead*'s zombies are wonderfully real?"

"No! They're hokey! But they *think* they're realistic!"

"So they take themselves too seriously?" I ask.

"Yes!" The vein on his neck is pulsing. "Which is why *Zombies from Space* is awesome!"

I set aside my fuzzy feeling and keep arguing.

"I don't watch TWD for the zombies," I say. "They're frickin' cool. But they are not why I watch the show. I watch the show because of the characters."

"Yeah, but they drag it out," he says. "They're going to come to the same realization as everyone else... the same blatant answer, but they're taking six seasons to get there!"

"Which is what?"

"You do what you have to do to survive."

"Of course that's the answer!" I say. "But it isn't the point. Of course they are going to do what they have to do to survive. We watched this develop in Carol. We saw it lost in Morgan. And that's really what he's afraid of! Morgan is convinced that if he kills again, he'll go back to doing whatever he must to survive. Something his therapist failed to cover with him. We see this strong in Rick. Survive. Of course! Crossing the lines of humanity? Most definitely! But at what cost? And that's the question. Survival has a price and while humanity has fallen apart around them, Rick and his group desperately hang onto theirs. While it's taken us six years to get this far, it's really only about two years in their time."

"But that's just it!" my scientist shouts. "The human body falls apart after a few weeks."

"But it isn't about the zombies," I shriek. "They're just cool. The point isn't survival. The point is humanity during apocalypse. This is like watching *Apocalypse Now* in slow motion. But at what point will their need to survive and end their humanity? At what point will it break them? At one point will they too join the cannibals, rapists, and wolves? Can they embrace survival and keep their humanity?"

I get a pensive grunt. He thinks for a moment and goes back to his science fiction novel.

So here we are: *Zombies from Space... and Vampires.* I had to come up with a credible explanation, one that my husband would accept... one that would stand against scientific accuracy.

What if the zombies are an alien race who just happen to resemble zombies? What if their food source is humanoids? What if they come from a planet with a much lower gravitational pull and their cell division rate is exceptionally faster than ours? So that they are constantly shedding their bodies every few days, but when placed on Earth, where the gravitational pull is much higher, their flesh and skin is ripped off of them like rags, giving them the appearance and movement of zombies.

It was sound. My scientist approved the science. It was credible enough that he could accept the claim of zombies.

So I have my "zombies." I have my apocalypse. But then I had an idea. How could I make this even more epically awesome? Vampires! And that is when I realized the zombies would threaten the vampire food source. Zombies versus vampires. That was the original title. But I couldn't let go of "Zombieeeees... from SPACE!" Aliens. Zombies. Vampires. What more could you ask for?

# Chapter One

***Drip** the drops of golden light in the black of night.*

Nineteen-year-old Aria Danes peered up from the line scrawled in her notebook. The rain rolled down the window of the mobile home, and the orange of the street lamp reflected through the droplets streaking the glass. Aria sighed and gazed at the clock. Two o'clock. Her father would be done with his shift soon.

The diner was always dead this time of night.

*"Cost more to keep the lights on and the staff there than it ever was worth,"* her father frequently grumbled. *"My father boasted a twenty-four-hour diner for forty-eight years as did his father before him. Ain't gonna change that now."*

Her father quoted the words of his employer all too well. Aria would chuckle and her father would slip the baseball cap on his balding gray head and, giving Aria a hug, would head off across the parking lot to work.

Aria loved the mobile home. It was cozy, ideal, and practical. With just her and her father and a constant set of wheels under their feet, they were always ready to go... if ever they could save enough to get gone. Her father, Richard Danes, was a down-to-earth, hard-working average man of forty-something. He had spent the last ten years trading strands of hair for the wisdom it took to raise his small family, which was always only Aria. Their mother had taken off years ago and died, all before Aria had learned how to miss her.

She wasn't missed as Mr. Danes was always there to be whatever it was that Aria needed that day. Their existence was simple and, at nineteen years, all Aria wanted to do was get gone from the small one-light town and move on to bigger places.

"Go to college," Mr. Danes would nag with a smile. "Be something better than me."

Matching his grin, Aria always retorted, "I am something better."

Before he could argue, Aria would go back to her dreams set to the songs on her iPod.

Aria sat up from the window at the sudden tap on the glass. Through the black and orange streaks of rain, her father smiled up at her. Aria opened the window.

"I'll be along later than I thought," Mr. Danes said. "The boss wants to go over staffing tonight."

"Tonight?" Aria whined.

"He says it will be nice and quiet then. Best time."

Dejected, Aria nodded.

"What are you still doing up, anyway?" Mr. Danes asked.

Aria shrugged. "Couldn't sleep."

"Well. . . " Mr. Danes looked back at the diner to hide his smile. "Too much like your father."

Aria leaned out of the window and kissed the top of his head.

"Right," she said. "Night, Dad."

The rain was picking up again.

"You're not going to sleep, are you?" Mr. Danes asked.

"Nope." Aria flashed him her favorite grin. "Too much like my father."

"Stubborn," he said, turning back to the diner. "I'll see you when I'm done."

The rain had most definitely started up again. A downpour was well on its way.

"Bye, Dad," she said.

Mr. Danes waved good bye and, crouched under his coat, ran through the muddy parking lot back to the diner.

Aria fought the mobile home window, which had jammed again. The thing was always sticking. The wind picked up and, just as Aria gave the window a punch to dislodge the misaligned frame, a sharp whistle cut through the night and the rain suddenly stopped.

Richard Danes had just made it to the end of the parking lot where the diner's cheap fluorescent lights flickered. He looked back at the mobile home. The window forgotten, Aria leaned out of the window and cocked her head to better see the sky. It was too black, as if something had sucked out the light of the moon and the stars. Not even the outline of storm clouds was visible in the dark.

"Dad?" she called.

Dumbfounded, Richard looked around as if trying to determine where the rain had gone. He held a hand to his face, shading the street lamp light from his eyes to improve visibility.

"Dad?" Aria called. "What's happe—"

A second sharp whistle silenced Aria. Clasping her ears, she fell back, cringing against the sound as she lay huddled on the floor of the mobile home beside the foldout dining room.

Just as quickly, the shrill whistle stopped and the downpour continued.

Aria pulled herself to her feet and peered out the window. The rain fell as if nothing had been there moments ago to disrupt the downpour. Everything continued as it had before. Her father was gone.

"Dad?" Aria called over the rain. She gazed at the diner. The lights had gone out. It was silent. Everything was just too wrong. Worry pulled her nerves and Aria hugged herself against the gnawing fear that dug at her gut.

"Dad?"

Her pace increased with her rising panic as she made her way through the mobile home to the driver's cabin. Pushing open the door, Aria studied the parking lot for any sign of life.

Shadows moved in the distance. Aria strained to see through the rain and night at the movement ahead. A kind of distant gurgling followed and before Aria could scream, a kind of thing, ragged and limp, slogged through the mud. Its arms hung at its side like rags.

The stench hit her nose and, as she opened her mouth to scream, a cold hand clamped down around her and held her mouth closed.

"Not a word," a man's voice muttered in her ear. "Not a sound."

His cold slender fingers caressed her cheek as she breathed deep the stale scent of death.

"You don't know what that is, do you?"

Aria nodded. A strand of hair fell to her face.

"You do?" The man sounded surprised. "You know then what it will do if it gets you?"

The walking limp thing slogged toward Aria, who fought the hand keeping her in place. The man holding her ran a cold cheek against hers and breathed deep, as if smelling Aria.

"Nothing quite whets the appetite like frightened female," he said.

A sudden grunt from the left forced the man to shift, coming to face a second man-shaped thing slogging through the mud. Its arms also hung like shredded rags. Its stench bit Aria's nose. Up close in the streetlamp's light, Aria could see the shredded remains of rotting corpse. She screamed into the hand that held her mouth as the dead thing reached for Aria. Releasing a silky laugh, the man stepped again, taking Aria with him just as the walking corpse lunged. With a swipe of his arm, a blade flew up and took the corpse's hand with it. The man holding Aria shifted and she broke free.

Stumbling, she ran away from the man and the slogging corpse and stopped at the wall of moving shadows that limped toward her. Still alive, the armless corpse hissed at the man with the sword. Too frightened to move, she watched as the man swept his sword across the dead, taking its head with it.

"Now then," he said, straightening his vest as a snarling body behind Aria fell on her. Before Aria could gasp, the man was beside her with his blade forced through the dead. This close, Aria could see the perfect pale skin of the man, with thick black hair sleeked back. Eyes as black as death peered down at her. Eyes that Aria fell too deeply into pinned her in place. And just as quickly as the man had moved beside her, he was down on Aria, his lips on her neck.

A twinge of pain, her body weakened, and she fell into the man's cold arms as everything around her went black.

Aria woke in a dark room lavished in mahogany and blood red velvet. Despite the ache that strained each joint, Aria shoved back a heavy silk blanket that matched the red and sat up from the bed lined with four intricately carved bed posts. Based on the pain from her shoulder, a collection of bruises accompanied the strain in her joints.

An orange light spilled under the door and across the carpet. Distant voices in the adjoining room challenged the silence. Aria pushed herself from the bed. While she slept, someone had dressed her in a white nightgown that fell to her bare feet when she stood. Despite the lack of chains or bars, she was sure she wasn't free. Aria crept toward the door.

"What news?"

Aria almost opened her mouth to answer when a second voice, smooth like the first, cut her off.

"They've positioned themselves globally. . . strategically, from the looks of things." The second voice maintained a hint of worry. Quietly, Aria moved closer, desperate to hear every word, though they made no attempt to talk privately.

"And their progress?" This was the voice of the swordsman who had held her, back by the diner.

"They've already wiped out the governments, their armies, and the media."

"Leaders, defenses, communications. . . all in one move," the swordsman muttered.

"In a single night, from the looks of it. They're taking over," said the second. "Most cities have already been overrun. Others have been wiped out completely."

There was a pause as the silence settled.

"How much time?" the swordsman asked.

"If we leave them to their plans?" Aria imagined a defeated shrug she couldn't see. "Few weeks. Maybe a month. That depends on how proactive the humans decide to be."

"Humans," Aria breathed, then held her breath.

"Is no one left?" the swordsman said. "Has anyone made any decisions to move?"

"From the looks of it, they had no time," the second voice said. "Everything is already gone. The Weeches were thorough."

Aria had no idea what that meant, but the worried sick she had at the diner was back stronger than ever.

"That doesn't leave us much choice," the swordsman said. There was a hint of defeat in his tone. "Round them up."

"My lord."

Aria bit down on her fist. Despite the barrage of questions and confusion, she was certain "them" meant humans and she was doubly sure that whoever or whatever "they" were, they were the rotting bodies that had surrounded her.

"Come out," called the swordsman. "I know you heard every word."

Making up her mind to stand tall, Aria pushed against the door that opened into a lavish sitting room. The rich mahogany and blood red velvet continued into this room.

A red lounger rested as the centerpiece before a crackling fireplace encased in stone. Despite the number of candelabras, wall sconces, and candlesticks, only a handful were lit. Lavishly carved sofa tables lined the walls that dripped with velvet drapes.

*Strange,* she thought over the obscene lack of electrical lights.

Beside the lounger's end, the swordsman stood. Behind him a pair of tall doors rose to the ceiling: the door of her cell. Aria looked back to her host. The pair of black eyes stared back. Set within a perfectly pale complexion, Aria could now see her captor clearly. His black hair was sleeked back and hung long down his neck. He was tall and thin, but clearly strong. . . and powerful. She had no doubt about the power harbored within his body. That was made very clear from where he stood. Aria assessed his full height at a few inches over six foot. He towered over her own five foot four inches.

"Where is my father?" Aria asked, getting right to the only question that mattered.

"Your father?" the swordsman repeated.

"My father." Aria's words were dangerously close to shouting, but she held back. She wasn't about to show him emotion. She had already decided he wasn't worth it.

"For the life of me, I truly don't know," he answered too politely.

Aria decided not to push the issue just yet.

"What do you want?" she asked, forcing the question.

"A few things," he answered then paused, taking a moment to look her up then down.

Visibly repressing a grin, he assessed her as if deciding her fit to ogle.

"Your question is vague," he finally answered.

"Who are you?" Aria asked, slightly miffed at his admiration.

"Better." He permitted a full grin to expand his mouth as his eyes shone with a satisfied gleam. "I am Caius."

"Why am I here?"

"I brought you here." Caius said this as if he had done her a favor.

"What were. . . " Aria hesitated. All the words that came to mind were ludicrous. Downright foolish.

"Zombies?" Caius finished for her.

"Oh, don't say it," Aria groaned. The whole thing was ridiculous. She grimaced, showing the first sign of emotion since she woke. Knowing better, she cursed herself and recomposed her cool head.

Caius chuckled. "Not quite zombies, though they do look the part, don't they?"

Aria stared with a disapproval she barely kept in check. None of this amused her and she wasn't in the mood for games.

"What you saw was an invasion," Caius said, circling the lounger. He settled himself onto the couch. Resting his arm across the back of the lounger, he crossed his legs. "The first of many. While you slept, nearly fifty more have landed—"

"Landed?"

"Your race is being wiped out."

The blood drained from Aria's brain and she felt herself sway.

"W—" She couldn't speak.

"Have a seat," Caius said, pointing to the place beside him. "You haven't eaten in days."

"Days?" Aria focused her attention back on Caius. "How long was I—"

"Three days, Aria."

"How do you know my name?"

"You must be hungry."

At the mention of food, Aria noticed the ache in her belly and how small her stomach felt. Based on the curve of her trim torso, she assumed she had lost almost ten pounds in those few days.

"I'll have something brought up from the kitchens," Caius said, standing from the couch.

"Where am I?" Aria asked.

"You're safe."

"I'm going." Aria announced and, selecting the nearest route to the doors, brushed past Caius. She had made it a whole two steps before he was on her, in front of her, holding her. Aria had no time to respond. Caius was close, his mouth on her neck.

His breath grazed her ear.

"Chains and bars don't hold you because we don't need them," he breathed, touching his lip to her ear.

Cold slid down Aria, and with it, an understanding. The power she had felt from Caius was no illusion. She felt it in his arms. With no effort, he could snap her in two and very little kept him from doing so. She doubted he would feel remorse for the action. If Caius wanted, nothing stopped him from taking her. That was made very clear as he placed a gentle kiss to the edge of her ear and, still holding her at the waist, permitted her a step back.

*Permitted.*

"You have much to learn, Aria," Caius whispered. "Xavier."

Aria remained frozen as Xavier opened one of the vast doors enslaving her.

"Have the kitchens prepare something for Miss Danes," Caius said. His request was polite and kind because, Aria was certain, he didn't have to be anything else. She heard the same compliance in Xavier's voice as before.

"My lord." Xavier bowed and closed the door behind him.

Aria gazed at Caius's face and studied the callous emptiness there.

"Your heart is black," Aria said. "I see it in your eyes."

Caius smiled proudly as if swept away by her. Before Caius could answer, Aria took her gaze from Caius and marched back to her room, slamming the door between then.

The chamber was bold and bleak. Even the fire in the hearth felt cold despite the dancing flames casting orange about the room.

"Well, this is creepy," Aria muttered, gazing at the red drapes, matching linens, and thick plush carpets as deep a red as crimson blood. She hugged herself, rubbing her arms as one of the thick curtains moved. Aria paused a moment then bolted toward the open window hidden behind the curtain. She threw open the drapes and gasped.

The window was in fact a set of glass French doors left open to a stone balcony. Aria stepped out onto the terrace. From the terrace, she could see just what her prison was: a Gothic castle complete with crenelated stone parapets nestled on an island somewhere.

Night blanketed the world in beautiful black, save for the moon above, as clear and perfect and whole as ever. Ahead was a river so wide as to hide the horizon behind the shadows. The shadows that moved. Aria focused her attention on the line of black in the far of distance then gasped, her hand on her mouth. There, beyond the abstract of imagination, Aria could see the sloth movement of each zombie. As far as the eye could see, millions roamed like an infectious cancer that had seeped over the land and spread.

A harsh crash jerked Aria back from the horror and she spun around in time to see a small woman in an English frock from the 18th century. She was dangerously thin, almost clumsy as she straightened a silver tray laden with what looked like the fixings of a lavish meal. Salted beef, red wine, ripe cheeses, and fruits dressed the platter. She lost her appetite though when a cold, gentle hand touched her shoulder. She didn't have to see him to know Caius stood behind her.

"Leave us, girl." Caius's silky voice climbed her spine.

Aria moved to take a step as the English maid bumbled off. In a hurried state, she closed the doors behind her as if too frightened to raise her eyes from the floor. Aria turned to face Caius.

"I had a platter brought up for you." His voice was too soft.

"Do you really expect me to thank you?"

"It would be nice," he purred.

"Thank you," she sneered.

"You're welcome." Caius smiled. In the moonlight, like this, she could too easily make out the fine white rows of his teeth, and the over-pronounced canines that were only visible with a full smile.

With an amused scoff, Aria shook her head. "What is this?"

Caius tipped his head in question.

"You can't possibly expect me to believe that they. . . " Aria motioned toward the window.

"The zombies?" Caius finished for her.

"Ugh." Aria felt her stomach flip with the stupidity of it all. "And that you. . . " She looked Caius up then down.

Overall, he was quite stunning to look at. She would have found herself flirting shamelessly had she not been so worried about her father or the fact that she was standing in a 17th century Dracula mock-up, and a rather convincing one too. She wasn't sure what she was trying to say.

"And what am I?" Caius asked.

"I don't have to answer that," Aria said.

Caius inhaled and took a step toward Aria, who raised her head in defiance. She refused to stand down.

*All he has to do is move, and he can break you.* She repeated the mantra over as she stood tall. He was so close she could smell his sweet musk and feel the power he harbored, so close that her chin nearly grazed his chest.

"You are quite beautiful," Caius whispered and slid a finger down her jaw.

Aria slapped it away.

"If you don't mind, my dinner's getting cold," Aria said.

"As is mine."

Aria stiffened.

"I can wait," Caius said, heading for the door. "I'm not getting any older."

With a subtle bow, as if to bid her good night, he closed the door behind him.

# Chapter Two

Aria ran toward the door and yanked on the handle. Convinced it was locked, she stumbled back a bit when it swung open. She recovered her balance and poked her head into the sitting room. Caius was gone.

*Of course he is,* she mused.

Without hesitation, Aria closed the door. With how fast he could move, she was certain he was watching. If she was going to escape, it would have to be planned. Thought out. Carefully plotted.

"Hey."

Aria all but jumped out of her skin and turned to a woman lounging too comfortably on an armoire shoved into the shadows against the stone wall. The umbra masked most of her presence, but not enough that Aria couldn't make out the slender body wrapped in form-fitted black leather. Slick leather boots stopped at her knees, and her lush brown hair dyed purple with subtle blue tips touched her thighs. The woman affectionately clutched a flask with a sleek manicure that left her nails painted black. Their sheen was striking in the shadow touched by slivers of moonlight as she tipped the flask back for a drink.

From the smell, Aria was certain she was chugging Merlot.

"Who are you?" Aria asked.

"Call me Cin," she said, putting the stopper on the flask and casually shoving it into her boot.

"Sin," Aria repeated. "Are you one of them?" Aria asked a bit snarkier than intended.

Cin slid down from the armoires.

"Hardly," she said. "No."

"What are they?" Aria asked. "Where am I? Do you know where my father is?"

"Vampires, or the closest thing to what you would call vampires, the Saint Lawrence River, and no. I don't know where your father is," Cin said.

Paying no mind to the first two answers, Aria's shoulders dropped. She dug her hands into her eyes and crushed the tears that burned there.

"Are you alright?" Cin asked.

"I don't. . . " Aria was running out of shock. She felt her strength wane and, as her body began shaking, she started crying. Any moment now she would fall to the floor blubbering.

"Hey," Cin said, gently hushing Aria. "You're okay. Here." Cin pulled a second flask from the inside of her purple-black leather jacket. Accepting the flask, Aria threw back one long gulp, expecting the dry, thick body of a Merlot.

A moment later, she was hunched over in a fit of coughs.

"What—" More coughs cut Aria off. "—is this?"

"Absinthe," Cin said.

After a moment, Aria's coughing calmed down enough for her to stand upright again.

"Better?" Cin asked.

Aria nodded with a final cough.

"Good. Ready to go?"

"Go?" Aria asked as Cin walked to the terrace.

"Unless you want to stay here." Cin paused, as if unsure what Aria wanted. "Do you?"

"No," Aria said.

"Alright then. This way."

Aria followed Cin to the terrace and looked down where a long nylon rope was secured with something that resembled climbing equipment. Aria studied the rope system with question.

"We have a guy who works for us. This is one of his own creations. Frickin' awesome if you ask me."

Aria nodded her understanding and listened to the instructions Cin gave as she secured the pulley system to her waist.

With Cin leading the way, Aria followed suit.

"You'll kick and slide," Cin said.

Aria nodded. "Kick and slide."

Cin was already on her way down. A moment later, her feet touched the ground.

"Ready?"

Aria took a deep breath. "I got this."

A cold hand slammed down on Aria's, holding her there on the terrace. Gasping, Aria looked up into Caius's eyes.

"Going somewhere?"

"Aria, let go!" Cin called.

But Caius had his fingers twisted in Aria's hair.

"Aria!" Cin cried.

Before Aria could call out, Caius was on her. His teeth sunk into her neck. Aria battled a surge of dizzy sleep as her grip relaxed on the rope.

"Shit," Cin said from the ground. "Aria, let go!"

But already Aria was unconscious and asleep in Caius's arms.

Pulling a small contraption from her belt, Cin snapped her wrist and the contraption unfolded into what looked like a child's flying toy. Cin threw the device. Propelled by internal mechanics, it sailed up to the terrace. The climbers' equipment released itself from the balcony at the same moment that the device released a line of electricity that fired at Caius's chest and held him there.

Crying out in pain, Caius released Aria and she fell.

"Aria!" Cin yelled, watching Aria fall from the terrace.

Before she could move to break Aria's fall, a flash of black pulled Aria from the air.

Standing besides Cin, a woman, clad all in black, held Aria. Fishnet stockings grazed her legs between the platform-heeled leather boots and the leather miniskirt. The bottom half of her black hair had been dyed with such deep a red that her hair looked like it dripped blood. Her black lips parted with a coy smile, making her already beautifully cold skin all the paler. Dark eyeliner enhanced the mischief in her gaze as Aria began to waken, still in a haze.

"Kylie!" Caius called down from the terrace. "Bring her here."

Kylie gave an amused scoff. "Make me," she said, earning a pursed snarl from Caius.

"Here," Kylie said, passing Aria to Cin.

"Kylie!" Caius shouted.

Kylie flipped a finely manicured finger at Caius. Her black polish caught the moonlight.

"Back down, Kylie," Caius warned.

"Blow it out your hole," Kylie said.

As Cin helped Aria find the ground beneath her, there was a flash from the balcony and, gasping, she braced for an impact that never came. Behind her Kylie stood, the only barrier between Cin and Caius. Kylie's outstretched arm pushed against him.

"Watch your sides, little sister," Caius said.

"Watch yours."

Caius growled.

"You better get going," Kylie said to Cin. "If he gets mad enough, I won't be able to stop him."

As Cin began to move away with Aria, Caius attempted to shift around Kylie, but Kylie moved too fast. Her hands slammed into Caius's chest, blasting him back several feet. He regained his balance and moved to shift again, but in the time that it took Caius to recover, Cin and Aria were gone.

"Wench!" Caius said, raising his hand to strike Kylie. She caught his fist.

Kylie smiled as Caius ground his teeth.

"I never should have pulled you back," he said.

"No," Kylie said. "You shouldn't have."

Caius pulled back his hand.

"I could have you killed here," he threatened.

"No," Kylie said. "You can't or you would have ages ago."

Without another word, Kylie sauntered on toward the gardens, away from the castle and Caius.

"Get in my way again, Kylie, and you won't survive the day."

Kylie began to whistle a tune of her own making.

"There are other ways to kill an immortal who refuses to die!"

"We'll see," Kylie said, not bothering to look back.

"Trollop!" Caius shouted and Kylie gave a nonchalant wave from the gardens, her manicured nails with the black sheen catching the moonlight.

# Chapter Three

**C**in dropped Aria into the small rowboat that rocked against the water. Taking up an oar, she pushed against the land and set the boat in motion away from the island.

Aria stirred, wincing as she shifted herself uncomfortably in the boat.

"Take it easy," Cin said.

"I'm. . . " Aria tried to answer.

"We're alright now," Cin said.

"Where are we. . . "

"On the Minnow," Cin said.

". . . going," Aria clarified.

Cin gave a contented smile and pulled a flask from her back pocket before throwing down a drink.

"Somewhere safe," said Cin.

The boat made its way upstream, cutting through the night fog. Aria hugged her knees to her chest, her attention only fixed on the walking corpses slogging their way along the bank of the river.

"What are they?" Aria said.

"They're zombies," Cin said, half smirking.

Aria frowned at Cin.

"No, I mean. . . really."

Smiling, Cin raised her flask to her mouth.

"What happened?" Aria asked.

Another long drink.

"What does it look like?" Cin asked at last.

Aria stared through the fog at a collection of corpses hunched over, taking turns pulling the flesh off a screaming woman. Aria winced as Cin chugged back another drink.

"How did you find me?" Aria asked.

Cin shrugged.

"Do you know anything?"

Cin didn't miss the bite in Aria's tone.

"I know plenty," Cin said. "I just don't think I'm the one to explain, nor is a boat in the middle of the Saint Lawrence River the place to break the news to you."

Aria stared at the shore and watched the run of corpses trudge along upstream. Screams followed them through the night as the moon filled the sky. Shadows thickened. Now and then, Cin gave a push off with the oar, allowing the current to carry them.

The soft lapping against the boat lulled Aria into a dulled rest; Cin's composure brightened.

"There," Cin said pointing ahead.

Aria followed Cin's enthusiasm and gasped at the large vessel dead ahead.

"A boat?" Aria said.

Cin chuckled. "Don't let the Captain hear you call it a boat."

"Captain?" Aria said, and Cin smiled.

"Aye, the Captain. She's a ship," Cin said. "And that be the HMS Slush Brain."

They drew near the ship. The port holes blazed with orange. On board, Aria could make out the occasional lantern that appeared to be swinging on deck. The closer they got to the ship, the more the fog cleared until

Aria could make out a black silhouette. The pigtails that framed a head were dwarfed by the rocket launcher perched casually on a shoulder. The blood drained from Aria's face as the snap of pink bubblegum broke the silence.

"What be on board the deck tonight?" a voice from the deck carried down.

"Just a Slush Brain filled with pirates, the booze, and the bitter bite of black powder."

The girl lowered the rocket launcher as the boat drew closer. The swaying lantern cast an occasional light on a woman sporting a long set of blond and pink pigtails.

Cin grinned up at the woman dressed like a Catholic child, who blew a pink bubble. Smiling down at The Minnow, she said one word.

"Amazeballs."

"Hello, Stani!" Cin said, smiling up at the deck where the woman with the blond and pink pigtails stood, the rocket launcher still resting on her shoulder.

"Captain's been worried for you, Cinders," the woman said.

"Tell her to grab a Guinness and relax," Cin said. "I'll be there soon enough. Help me get Aria on board."

The woman on deck threw down a rope ladder. Using the ladder, Cin pulled the boat parallel with the ship.

"Come up," Cin said to Aria, who stood too quickly and rocked the wee boat too violently.

"Hold now," Cin said, grabbing Aria's arm to steady her. "Of all the rivers to swim in, you don't want to go falling into this one." Cin passed Aria the rope ladder. "Here. Go on up first. Stanushka will be up there to greet you."

Aria looked up at Stanushka just as her pink bubblegum popped. Stani smacked her lips, pulling the gum back in her mouth, and chewing in delight as she smiled down at Aria.

"Right," Aria said and pulled herself up the ladder.

"Here," Stani said, lowering the rocket launcher to her side. She reached down and took Aria's hand.

"Welcome on board the HMS Slush Brain, Aria," Stani said. "You're going to love it here."

Cin pulled herself over the gunwale and hopped down to the deck with ease.

"You drink?" Cin asked.

"What?" Aria asked, turning to Cin who was already pulling a flask from her other boot.

"Here."

Aria shook her head as Cin threw down a drink.

"You'll need it. Where's the Captain, Stani?"

"With the guys," Stani said. "This way."

Only when Stani stooped to retrieve a second weapon resting on the deck did Aria notice the flintlock long-barreled gun tucked affectionately at Stani's side along with a Dillinger nestled into her leather boot that stopped at her thighs.

"What's with the artillery?" Aria muttered to Cin.

"Hm? Stani? Stanushka loves the firearms," Cin said. "Don't you, Hawaii?"

"Yep!" Stani said.

Aria studied the gun in Stani's right hand. "Isn't a flint-lock rather slow for the times?"

"You watch your mouth," Stani said with a stern look over her shoulder. "This isn't an ordinary flintlock," she said and led Aria and Cin through a door below the upper deck.

Tucked beneath the upper deck, a warm welcoming light filled a small but cozy room that served as kitchen, dining room, and social room in one. All the makings of a kitchen lined the farthest wall where a short woman—wearing a white gown, tiara, and pirate hat—stood hunched over as she combed through the fridge.

On the opposite side of the fridge, a tall Scandinavian, dressed too well in leather and swords that dripped from his body, rested his arm on the open fridge door. His long blond hair fell well past his shoulders, and the beard made him look too much like a warrior who had stepped from the pages of *Beowulf*. The great sword on his back and the scimitar at his waist added to the look of Swedish warrior. Wide shoulders and large arms confirmed his constant use of the blade.

A tall man with fine hands sat at the table. Fidgeting with something that resembled clockwork, he sat hunched over, oblivious to all else in the room. His only earring caught the light as he paused to adjust his monocle. He slipped his hand into one of the pockets tucked away in his colorful gold vest and withdrew something so minute, Aria couldn't identify it.

"Hi." The Scandinavian smiled from the fridge. "I'm Norry."

"Where's my Guinness?" the woman in the fridge shouted.

"You drank it, Ange," Norry said, then smiled at Aria, as if proud. "She's the Captain. This is our captain."

"I didn't. You took—"

Aria steadied herself on the back of a chair.

"You drank the last bottle yourself," Norry said.

A sickness rose in Aria. Her head spun worse than ever.

"Guys," Stani said.

Norry and Angela looked in time to see Aria start to drop and Norry jumped, catching her just before she hit the ground.

"When was the last time she ate?" Angela asked, forgetting the booze.

Aria held her head, unable to steady her nerves. The room was spinning, churning her stomach.

"You did drink my Guinness," Angela shouted quite suddenly at Norry. "I can smell it on you!"

"I didn—"

Vomiting, Aria sat up and bathed Norry in her insides. The last thing she heard before passing out was Angela's laughter.

# Chapter Four

Aria's head pounded with every creak. Consciousness flooded back as she noted the scent of cinnamon in the warm air. Aria moved. The last few hours, days, or weeks finally paid their toll and every joint screamed in protest. The taste of vomit lingered in her mouth as she attempted to sit up in the dark room.

"Slowly now."

Aria turned to the gentle voice and was greeted by Stanushka's bright smile.

"Where am I?" she asked.

"Below deck. Sorry about them," Stani said, rolling her eyes as if embarrassed. "The Captain tends to forget there are others who aren't used to the zombies—"

Dropping her throbbing head back to the bed, Aria released a groan.

"You don't like zombies?" Stanushka asked.

Aria was feeling sick again.

"I don't—" Aria pursed her lips. A wave of tears burned her eyes.

"Hey," Stani soothed in a sing-song voice. "You're alright."

Aria shook as she quietly cried.

"I know. . . " Stani said, rubbing Aria's arm. "It's a lot to take in at first."

"What—" Aria took a deep breath. "What happened?"

"You were sick, then you fainted, an—"

"No." Aria punched the bed. "What. Happened."

"Oh." Stani's shoulders dropped with understanding. "Yeah, I guess we didn't do a great job explaining things."

Aria stared at the ceiling as tears streamed down her face.

"We're being invaded," Stani said. "Well. . . have been invaded."

Aria turned to Stani, her mouth agape with shock.

"A year ago, the Office for Outer Space Affairs—or OOSA—received communications from an unidentified alien source," Stani said.

"Unidentified alien?" Aria repeated. "A year ago?"

Stani nodded. "Yes."

"And they didn't tell anyone?"

"Global panic, terror, chaos, religious zealots, apocalypse. . . Would you?"

Aria returned her gaze to the ceiling.

"OOSA kept it quiet," Stani said. "The public. The press. Governing bodies. . . " Stani shook her head. "No one knew about the Weeches except for the Office for Outer Space Affairs."

"Aliens," Aria repeated.

"Weeches," Stani said.

"Weeches."

"What you think are zombies, they aren't zombies at all. They're an alien race called Weeches."

"Of course they are," said Aria.

"It helps if you think of them as Weeches," Stani said. "When the Weeches arrived, OOSA kept things quiet and suggested a plan that would prepare the public for their reveal. The Weeches loved the idea and OOSA financed the Mission to Mars through NASA, which they planned to use for the Weech reveal."

"Weech reveal," Aria muttered.

"Things appeared to be going along to plan. The scheduled reveal was weeks away. Men had taken their first steps on Mars when one of the OOSA employees stumbled upon the Weeches' real agenda. The communications and negotiations were all a ruse. While OOSA danced like puppets, focused on trade agreements, negotiations, and the Mission to Mars, the Weeches were organizing a full-scale invasion hidden in the guise of peace and friendship. By the time the OOSA learned all of this, the Weeches had moved in. They took over everything all before anyone had grown wiser. They began with the military bases around the world, the media, and all governing bodies. Civilians were left with no defenses, no leaders, no communications, and no warning that this was coming. . . or that an alien race had even arrived."

"They took out our organized militia," Aria said as the words sunk in.

"And all communications. Television, news, complete stations. . . "

"The power of the media," Aria whispered.

"Of knowledge," Stani said. "By the time the government learned of the invasion, the media and militia were gone."

"They had no way to warn the public or prepare them," Arias said.

"Or protect them," Stani said.

"We were sitting ducks."

Aria's head spun as she tried to imagine the walking corpses as capable of establishing an undercover and discreet operation. "How could something like that sneak up on anything?"

"Those aren't the Weeches exactly," Stani said.

"Well then, what are they?" Aria sat up and spun her legs around so her feet touched the floor.

"We're not quite sure," Stani said. "OOSA fell before their research department made it that far."

"OOSA," Aria said. "If it went under, how do you know all this?"

"We have a crew member from OOSA," Stani said. "The Professor continues what he started with OOSA."

Aria sighed.

"The Professor thinks they are a kind of foot soldier responsible for harvesting on behalf of the Weeches. Or maybe their fighters... Maybe they really do look like that. We just don't have enough information yet," Stani said.

"Who are all of you?" Aria asked.

"Just a group of...well...we're kind of an assortment—"

"An imbroglio," Angela said, cutting Stanushka off. At the base of the steps, the Captain stood with an apple in hand. "A confused mass. Sorry we came off strong," Angela said, handing the apple to Aria who accepted the fruit. Within a few large bites, the apple was gone. "We are whipping something up in the kitchens for you. Feeling better?"

Aria nodded.

"When was the last time you ate something?" Angela asked.

"The night my father..."

A lump stoppered Aria's words and she dug her fist into her brow.

"What happened the night you lost your father?" Stanushka asked.

Aria thought back to that night.

"It was raining," she began. "Pouring, actually. Then it stopped... suddenly like—" Aria shook her head. "Like something paused the rain. There was a whistle. It was so loud... It hurt so much, I fell. When I looked out the window, it was pouring again, but... my father was gone."

"And you saw no one?" Angela asked.

Aria shook her head.

"How did you end up on Singer Island?"

"Singer..." Aria stopped.

"Singer Island," Angela repeated. "Yes. With Caius and his clan."

"Who..." Aria thought back to the night she met Caius. She truly had no idea how she came to be there when she woke or where even there was. "I don't know," she said. "After my father vanished, I was alone... but the... Weeches... They came and... I would have been dead if..."

Aria couldn't say the word. 'Vampire' sounded just as ludicrous as 'zombie.'

"Caius was there," she continued. "He saved me."

"He didn't save you," Angela said. "He was saving his dinner."

Aria hugged her stomach, wishing it would stop flipping.

"I've been to Singer Island," Aria said. "Once. Years ago. It was crawling with tourists and brides. Not Dracula."

"Same difference," Angela said. "When the Weeches invaded, Caius moved in and cleaned house. We think he liked the Gothic look of the place. Made him feel right at home."

"I don't..." Aria dropped her head into her hands. "Did Caius come in then with the Weeches?"

Angela and Stanushka exchanged a look.

"Perhaps we should see if dinner is ready," Angela said. "Stani?"

"Captain."

"Let's show her the boots."

"Boots!" Stani squealed. She was up in a moment. Her gun hung affectionately at her side. "Oh! Aria! You're going to love this! Let's get you out of the granny gown and into some leather!"

# Chapter Five

"**W**e are part of a small group that hunts Caius's clan," Angela said.

"Slayers," Aria confirmed, pulling a pair of black jeans over her hips.

"Vampire is the best way to describe what Caius is, but vampire is only the stories that developed over centuries to describe what he really is. Mortals' explanation for something they don't understand."

"So then, what is Caius. . . really?"

"They don't drink blood, if that's what you're asking," Angela said with a grin. "They are cannibals, kind of. They would be if they were human. There are no silver bullets, no garlic, no crosses or holy water. Those were superstitions developed by religious men who turned to their gods to protect them. And garlic was once used only as a standard medicine to treat a range of ailments."

"They thought it was a disease," Aria said, pulling on a pair of black leather boots she then zipped up the inside of her legs.

"Exactly. They do lack a tolerance to light, but that is because of where they live and their evolution and not because of what they are. They do not turn dead. No bats.

No coffins. Caius is immortal. He and his clan just. . . don't age. But they can be killed as easily as you or I."

"If there really are vampires, then why don't we know about them?" Aria asked.

"We did once," Angela said. "Mortals are terrified of that kind of power. So we specialized in hunting them down and killing them. They would have gone extinct if they didn't go into hiding and encourage the stories that we know today."

"Then why—"

"Because Caius has us at a disadvantage. He has centuries of training under his belt. While we only have one lifetime to master any one field, Caius has an infinite number of lifetimes. His clan has had the time to master every skill known to man. That puts him at a slight advantage."

"But. . . " Aria's hands went to her neck. Two pair of small punctures had scabbed over, but there was no denying what she had seen.

"The canines," Angela said. "That's what gave birth to most of the rumors. They don't use them to drink blood like bats. We all had canines once. Over the years, we evolved and our canines diminished. Theirs didn't. The canines are venomous—"

"Like snakes," Aria deduced.

"Yes. The venom paralyzes their prey. That's all. It renders them unconscious for. . . easy dining." Angela smiled at the thought and Aria swayed. The room was still spinning. "Those with allergic reactions have died from the venom. Hence the rumors. And an antidote can be made. . . just like an antidote for snake venom. In fact, that's what the Professor is working on now."

"Where is the Professor?" Aria asked.

The crew exchanged silent glances that convinced Aria to change the subject.

"But. . . don't you need the venom to create an antidote?" Aria asked.

She slid her arms through the ribbed sleeves of a black leather jacket and freed her hair.

"Yep," Angela said. "And therein lies our problem."

"And the solution," Norry said quite suddenly.

Aria looked over her shoulder at the bearded Scandinavian standing on the stairs.

"Dinner's ready."

# Chapter Six

The sound of food shoved all curiosity from Aria's mind about the problem and solution of a vampire venom antidote. Instead, she all but ran to Norry, who led Aria to the deck.

The night sky greeted Aria, giving a clear view of the stars. Aria gasped at the sheer volume of light that speckled the black canopy.

"It took some getting used to," Cin chimed in. "When the invasion hit, we lost power within the first week. The silence that followed. . . the lack of city light. . . "

Norry opened the kitchen door and the smell of roasted pork hit Aria hard. Her stomach tightened as she gulped down a mouthful of saliva.

"We'll eat," said Angela. "And then we'll review the plan.

The moment Aria stepped into the kitchen, Stanushka swept her into a chair at the table as plates filled up with pork and the brew was passed.

Norry, Stanushka, and Cin were at their places around the table with the monocled inventor who failed to pull his attention away from his work even for a moment to acknowledge that food was being served.

"Adam!" Angela called.

"Yo!" Adam answered, not looking up from his work.

"Eat! Take a break!"

Cin shoved a plate of pork beside him as she unstopped one of her flasks. The joyous clatter quickly filled the room as everyone dove in. Aria wasted no time filling her belly, and only when she forced herself to slow down did she glance around the table at the myriad of faces. A captain with a tiara, a purple-haired boozer dressed in leather, the blond with bubblegum pink tips. . . even here, an automatic flintlock had found its place at the table.

The Scandinavian swapped brews with Cin Dixon, who laughed easily. Through it all, Adam had found time to shove a bit of pork in his mouth despite his eye still being glued to his gadget, his monocle permanently fixed over his right eye. For a moment, Aria watched him reach a pair of fingers into a small pocket and pull out a gizmo she couldn't quite identify. Half-tweezers, half-magnifying glass, or perhaps a screwdriver. . . she couldn't tell.

He adjusted the monocle secured to his eye and kept working.

In less than twenty minutes, the pork had vanished. Save for a separate platter Stanushka was currently filling up, no other food remained. Aria watched Stani carry the plate to the counter.

"Now then," Angela continued. "The solution to our current dilemma—"

A cry cut the air and the cutlery froze. The crew exchanged silent glances. At the second distinct cry, everyone took up their nearest weapon and charged for the door. Too curious to inquire, Aria jumped to her feet and followed.

"Back! Back!" a man's voice screamed from the shore where only a black blur could be seen from a collected group. The gurgles and growls carried over the river from the bank.

"Away!" the man called.

A female voice screamed over the growls.

"Chess," Cin said, cueing the crew into action.

As smooth as glass, Adam casually kicked the side of the ship. A floorboard sprang up as the metal clank of anchor being dropped obeyed. Before Aria could inquire, Adam was down on a knee, withdrawing a large rocket launcher-styled something-turned-gadget from the deck. On beat, Adam aimed for the bank and squeezed the trigger, sending a grappling hook into the river's edge all as the ship came to a full stop.

As Aria collected her wits about the situation, Stani, Cin, and Angela had all equipped themselves and were already dropping a pulley-like contraption onto the rope that Adam had fired into the bank. With three zips, they were off. The subtle light clink of glass drew Aria's attention back to Adam, who was suddenly cradling a cup of tea. He slowly sipped the hot beverage as if savoring the bitter tannins and calm evening on the Saint Lawrence River set to moonlight and zombies. Aria looked to Norry, who was already leaning against the cabin wall nursing a waterskin that she suspected was filled with something stronger.

Adam adjusted his monocle.

"What are you doing?" Aria said. "Aren't you going to help them?"

"What for?" Adam said as if he was asking a student a pointed question about physics.

"Relax, Aria," Norry called. "They'll get pissed if we steal their fun."

# Chapter Seven

From the zip line, Stani fired her automatic flintlock and pelted the Weeches with buckshot. They took the hit, shuddering under the fire, giving the group time to touch down on shore and release themselves from the zip ties. Cin turned with her daggers leading the way. Weech guts spilled all over her hands as Angela unsheathed her swords and sliced her way into the crowd. Behind them, Stani fired off another round of buckshot.

As the Weeches took the hits, Cin and Angela made their way into the crowd.

"There!" Cin cried, burying her dagger into a Weech's skull and drawing Angela's attention to Chess "Cut Lass" carving out a hole around her.

"Who is that?" Angela asked as she took the head off a Weech. Cowering behind Chess, wearing nothing but a loincloth and black ragged boots, was a pale, scrawny man in the darkness. Aside from his index fingers positioned to form a cross, he seemed to do little else but release the occasional scream.

"Back!" he shrieked now, gathering enough courage to poke his head over Chess's shoulder.

With a new direction, Cin and Angela made their way toward Chess and the wild man. More Weeches swarmed, and Cin drove her daggers into necks, spilling cold spoiled blood over the ground. Stench engulfed them as Angela cut the legs out of another, driving her blades into skulls and guts. More Weeches came until a sounding pulse released through the crowd, knocking Chess, Angela, Cin, and the wild man to the ground.

As the smoke cleared, all they could see was Stanushka patiently waiting for everyone to rise. A bazooka was nestled affectionately on her shoulder.

"What?" Stani shrugged.

Cin and Angela climbed to their feet with Chess. Angela scrunched up her face.

"What smells like garlic?"

"Him," Chess said, pointing at the wild man still flat on his back, muttering madness beneath his breath.

The moonlight reflected off his chest and shone like a beacon in the middle of the night.

"What is he?" Cin asked, studying the wild man still lying flat on his back.

"Madness," he muttered. "Must. . . fight the madness."

Stani made her way through the Weech limbs and came to stand beside Chess, wearing 16th century pirate garb from buckled cuffed boots to pirate hat poised perfectly on black hair set with streaks of white.

"What is this, Chess?" Angela asked.

"Not sure," Chess said. "I found him on my run. He was stuck in a tree shouting stuff about the madness and the dark. It was all I could do to get a name out of him."

"Which is?"

"Matt," Chess said. "But I've taken to calling him Mad Matt."

Angela nodded approvingly. "It suits him."

"It does, doesn't it?"

"What's wrong with him?" Stani asked.

"Not sure yet," Chess said. "When the Weeches found him in the tree, he was crossing his fingers at them, shouting some crazy shit."

"He stinks like garlic," Angela said.

Chess frowned. "Yes. It's his loincloth. I think he soaked it in garlic butter. . . four months ago."

Mad Matt simply muttered at the stars as they spoke.

"The darkness," he muttered. "Darkness. . . the madness. . . and the darkness."

"Right," Angela said. "So, what do we do with him?"

"Well, we can't very well leave him here," Stani said.

"You aren't seriously proposing that we bring him on board the Slush Brain. . . "

"Well, look at him," Stani said. "He's kind of sweet."

In unison, the girls gazed down at the garlic-infested, near naked male splayed on the ground still panting to himself.

"Right-o," said Angela. "Bring him."

"The darkness. . . the madness. . . madness."

Aria studied the nearly naked man sprawled out on the lounger as he muttered endlessly in a thick English accent. He clutched the blanket to his chest as Adam moved a stethoscope over the man's chest.

"His eyes look like they're going to bulge right out of their sockets," Cinders announced as she settled down at the bar, clutching a wine bottle.

"They do, don't they?" Angela said.

"Darkness. . . "

"What's wrong with him?" Aria asked as Adam pulled the stethoscope from his ears and sighed.

"Well, nothing from what I can see. Whatever is wrong with him is mental."

"Clearly," Cinders said.

"Madness... Mad..."

"Has he said anything else?" Adam asked, contemplating the situation as if watching the machinations of a well-oiled contraption run.

"Nothing," Angela said. "He only talks about the darkness... and the madness..."

"And the darkness," Cin said.

"Right, that too," Angela said, not missing a beat.

"Hey." A loud crunch came from the door as Norry bit into an apple. "How's garlic boy doing?"

"Could you lot be any more insensitive?" Aria shouted as she jumped up from her spot at the counter.

Norry bit another loud chunk out of the apple.

"This poor man is clearly upset. Something has seriously messed him up—"

"You can say 'fuck,' Aria," Norry said.

"No!" Aria shouted. "I won't! I refuse to believe this situation is that bad! There are no vampires! There are no zombies—"

"Weeches."

"No!" Aria shrieked. "No Weeches! No vampires! No aliens and certainly no zombies!"

"Caius," Mad Matt suddenly whispered, drawing everyone's attention back to the lounger. "Caiu—"

In one swoop, Matt threw back the blanket and leapt to his feet. "Thou shalt not bring me back from the flames, you heathens! Devils! Not back from the darkness!"

Matt jumped from the lounger and before Cin could chug the rest of her wine, he was off running up the stairs to the main deck, three steps at a time, his garlic butter-soaked butt flap leaving behind a trail of stench.

"Liberty!" Matt screamed.

"Get him!" Chess shouted, drawing her cutlass and leading the series of whoops as Cin, Angela, Stanushka, and Chess bolted up the stairs after him.

Up the stairs, Matt led the menagerie that ran smack into his bare back at the top of the stairs.

"You," he growled, pointing a long finger at a figure standing on the deck of the Slush Brain.

"Be gone!" Matt shouted, but already Angela had drawn her sword. Cin, her daggers, and Stanushka had brought her rocket-launcher-styled contraption to her face and taken aim.

"Well, aren't you a sorry lot towing around that garbage now," came the lax drawl from the shadows. With ease, Kylie stepped from the gunwale to the deck. "You'd think we're at war or something."

"We are at war, sucker," Stanushka said.

"Right," Kylie said. "With the war and the Weeches and the blood. . . "

"What do you want, sucker?" Angela growled.

"Relax. I'm not here to help. I'm here to annoy," Kylie said. "And the easiest way to get under Caius's skin is to help you."

Everyone tightened their hold on their weapons.

"Caius will be coming for him," Kylie said, nodding at Mad Matt, who still stood terror-stricken. "If I were you, I'd get rid of him, lock him up, or run. Personally, I'd drown him, but that's me."

Angela looked the pasty male up then down. Rancid garlic butter dripped into his unlaced boots.

"Yeah, I know," Kylie said. "He doesn't look like much. But I assure you he wasn't always like that." With a skip in her step, Kylie was back on the gunwale. "I'd say you have an hour," she warned. "Caius doesn't like waiting."

With her next step, Kylie was gone, leaving behind only the lap of the water against the ship's strakes.

# Chapter Eight

"**W**e can't just sit here!" Stanushka shrieked below deck.

"We can take him," said Cin.

"What if she's lying?"

"Of course she's lying," Norry chimed in. "No woman who looks like that is an honest woman."

"You would know," Angela said.

"He's coming."

The soft sanity from Mad Matt was enough to shake the group into silence. Hunched in the corner, Matt peered up from his hand poised at his mouth as if he had taken in every word exchanged.

"And you know this?" Chess asked.

"He won't stop here," Matt said. "He'll destroy your ship. He'll kill all of you, rip you apart until the blood pours from your hearts. . . and then he'll eat it. . . he'll eat it. . . I know," Matt whispered. "I've seen him do it. . . to my sister. . . my mother. . . my wife. . . "

"Matt," Angela said, keeping her voice low.

Matt pushed the wet from his eyes.

"Kylie said you know something."

"Don't ask me that, love," he said. "Nothing 'bout that. I'm the only one who knows. And if anyone else knows, he'll come for you too."

"Matt," Stanushka said. "This information—what you know—will it help?"

"Don't ask, love," Matt said. He pushed a fresh wave of tears from his eyes and sighed. "I can't stay here."

As if resolved, Matt pushed himself to his feet and at once, grabbed a tool bag he spotted in a nearby corner. Randomly, he began walking through the room, tossing everything in sight into the bag.

Adam's tools—

"Uh. . . Excuse me?" Adam sputtered.

—a half-eaten sandwich from Norry's hands—

"Scuse you," Norry said.

—Cin's booze—

"Hey now," Cin growled.

—a pile of wood shavings from the floor where Angela had been whittling.

"Alright," Matt declared as if ready to undertake a great journey. He threw the last of the wood shavings into the bag and zipped it up with vigor. "I'll be off then. Cheerio."

"Now wait just a moment!" Angela shouted as Matt took up Angela's collector's edition *Doctor Who* scarf, with which he promptly attempted to dress himself.

An explosion on deck sent the Slush Brain into a fit of rocking, forcing everyone to grab hold of the tables, railings, and walls to stay upright.

"He's here," Matt said and, with tool bag in hand, fled up the stairs, the Doctor's fifteen-foot scarf trailing behind him.

"Not at sea, nor at bay will I sleep again," Matt howled as he ran up the stairs, plowing ahead with his head down and the bag tucked under his arm. Another bang, followed by a shower of debris, shielded Matt from view as he slipped behind the Captain's quarters and snatched a random wrench laying on top of a nearby barrel.

Another bang from the deck shook the ship, followed by a howl.

Matt grabbed a random gadget and ducked back behind the barrel.

"Captain!" Caius called over the bang.

One by one, Angela, Cin, Chess, Stanushka, Norry, and Adam spilled on deck, joining the horde of vampires all taking turns ripping the deck apart with a series of punches.

"My ship!" Angela screamed as Caius's minions took turns punching through the walls of the gunwale and kicking holes in the deck.

Stanushka raised the bazooka, Cin drew her daggers, and Chess cocked her guns and took aim.

"Captain!" Caius grinned.

"Caius," Angela said. "Get off my ship before I feed your heart to the Weeches."

"Tsk tsk," Caius said. "Such hatred."

"Now, Caius!"

"You have something of mine that I want, Captain. Give me back the girl. . . and the Doctor and we'll call things even. I and my kin will walk away, leaving your vessel intact."

"You'll walk away leaving the vessel intact regardless," Cin said.

Caius widened his grin. "Will I?"

Caius flinched and Stanushka fired the bazooka, missing Caius altogether as he sped across the deck toward the Captain. Caius reached for Angela's neck as she turned, sword in hand, to behead the first of Caius's minions. As the first of the heads fell to the deck, a small cloud of smoke burst in Caius's face, who snarled at the stench of beets.

Two more heads fell as Cin slashed with her daggers, turned, and crossed the blades across another throat. Beside her, Chess fired her flintlocks into the faces of oncoming vampires. They lunged with fingers as long as talons reaching to shred their prey. Bodies dropped to the deck as Norry took up his scimitar and severed the heads of vampires hissing up at him.

Recovered from the blast and stench of beets, Caius caught sight of Aria. Within a breath, Caius was on her from behind, his talons grazing her neck with a hungry grin.

"Your blood flows with venom, Aria. It's only a matter of time. . . "

"You touch her and your head will be next to fall," Angela said, her sword poised to Caius's throat.

"Don't wait, Captain. Kill him and be rid of him," Stanushka said. "Here. Let me help you." With her bazooka settled upon her shoulder, Stani peered down the scope at Caius.

"You know so little beyond your own eyes," Caius said.

"Hey, Caius!" Adam called from across the ship's deck. In his hand, he held something that resembled a child's top. "Go to hell."

Before he could release the top, a barrel of gunpowder exploded behind him, throwing Adam, his top, the crew, Caius, and his minions across the deck of the Slush Brain.

The top spun across the deck.

"No!" Adam said, but too late, it spun madly, releasing a cloud that smelled strongly of beets.

"Run," Adam said. Picking himself off the deck, he led the Captain and the crew overboard into the Saint Lawrence. Pushing his face off the deck, Caius watched the cloud mingle with the flames and burst into a chain of explosions that enveloped the ship in fire.

# Chapter Nine

"My ship!" Angela screamed from the water as pieces of the Slush Brain burst into shards and splinters of kindling. In silence, the crew and Aria gazed upon the wreckage, the last of their sanctuary consumed by fire and flame.

"Hey," a voice called to them from behind.

The crew turned to a small dingy rowed by Mad Matt. Still dressed in the scarf, Matt waved from inside the boat to signal to the crew, the black bag of random hodgepodge beside him.

"Ahoy!" he shouted.

The crew swam toward Matt's boat.

"Cin. Help Aria," Angela said.

Cin swam to Aria's side and lifted her into the boat.

"There you go, love," Matt said, pulling Aria out of the water.

"Here," Cin said, bracing her arms to pull herself in behind Aria. Already Stanushka was in the boat, helping Chess into the vessel, when something closed around Cin's ankle and pulled her back into the water.

"He—" Cin gulped in a mouthful of water.

"Cinders?" Stanushka asked, turning to where Cin had been a moment ago. Bubbles covered the surface.

"Cinders!" Stanushka cried.

Taking a deep breath, Angela dove under water.

From the bottom of the river, Weeches had spotted the crew. One had grabbed hold of Cinder's leg, pulling her down to the river's bottom. More Weeches swam toward Cin, who had managed to pull a dagger from her boot. But too late. A Weech grabbed Cin's wrist. Drawing her sword, Angela thrust the blade, piercing the Weech holding Cin's ankle through the chest. Almost instantly, the wound healed around Angela's blade.

Angela withdrew the sword, reopening the wound and spilling Weech entrails into the water.

An arrow with a modified head sailed through the water, severing the hand holding Cin's ankle. A second arrow severed the hand at Cin's wrist, buying her enough time to return to the surface as pieces of Weech spilled into the Saint Lawrence.

Standing up in the boat, Norry aimed a crossbow loaded with a third shot. Beside him, Stanushka loaded her crossbow.

The third arrow sailed into the chest of a Weech that grappled with Angela. It released the Captain, who swam to the surface. As Chess and Adam pulled Cin into the boat, Angela climbed out of the water. But the Weech, delayed by the impact, too quickly recovered and followed. Norry dropped to his knees, the crossbow abandoned, and punched the Weech in the face.

"Easy now," Adam soothed, patting Cin's back as she and Angela coughed oxygen back into their lungs. The surface of the Saint Lawrence settled as the Weeches returned to the river floor.

Air came back to Angela and slowly, she glared up at Matt, still wrapped in her vintage collector's edition *Doctor Who* scarf. Standing upright, she walked across the boat and punched Matt in the nose.

"Captain!" Adam said.

"Angela!" Chess cried.

"You blew up my ship!" Angela screamed as Matt held his bleeding nose. "Our home! Our weapons! All our supplies! Gone!"

"Angela," Cin eased. "How do you know he blew up the ship?"

"He was the only one missing on deck!" Angela screamed.

Silence followed as they all turned to Matt for an answer.

"Seemed like a good idea at the time," he said.

"Give me that," Angela said, taking back her scarf and leaving him in his boots and loincloth.

"So now what do we do?" Chess asked, averting the crew's attention to the dingy and few supplies surrounding them.

In the distance, the Slush Brain burned, lighting up the night with flame.

"Abandon ship," Angela said. "Those flames will draw in every Weech for miles. The sooner we get away, the greater our chances of slipping past the Weeches coming our way."

"We need a place to stay," Cin said.

"We need to conduct an inventory," Adam said. "See what supplies we have."

"We need food," said Stani.

The ship's mast creaked then snapped as it crashed into the deck of the Slush Brain.

"I know where we can go," Aria said.

One by one, the crew piled out of the boat onto land.

"Without weapons, we need to lay low," Angela said. "Any sound will draw the Weeches. Any movement will draw in Caius. We have little options and high priorities."

Balancing on Cin's firm grip, Aria clambered out of the boat with her new sea legs.

"When my father and I toured the Saint Lawrence, we found a marina," Aria said. "Cigar boats. Day cruisers. Tour ships... Any of these will be loaded with supplies."

"No telling how much has been stripped clean since the start, but it's worth a look," Norry said.

"That leaves weapons..." Cin said.

"Fort Drum."

All eyes turned to Adam, who straightened his monocle.

"We can hit up Fort Drum," he said.

"All the forts were taken," Chess said. "The military bases and forts were the first thing the Weeches hit."

"I checked the fort on my way to the Saint Lawrence," Adam said. "It was swarming with Weeches when I passed through, but it may be empty now. It could be stocked in weapons. It's worth a look."

"Any survivors in the area would have the same thoughts," Stanushka said.

"Food first. Then weapons," the Captain said. "Shelter."

"No matter where we settle, zombies or vampires," Cin said. "Take your pick."

"Oh, could we please not use the 'Z' word?" Aria cringed. "It makes this whole thing sound so stupid."

"What would you call them then?" Stanushka smiled. "Walkers?"

"Stalkers?" Adam suggested.

"Living Dead?" Chess added.

"My in-laws?" said Cin.

"Weeches is fine," Aria grumbled.

"Food first," Angela said. "Then we'll haggle about over our next roommate."

With bazooka in hand, Stanushka helped Norry and Adam pull the boat ashore. After shoving the dingy into the nearest bush, they buried it under a collection of branches.

"Come on," Angela said, waving the crew on. "Early morning is creeping in. In an hour, we'll have no mask from the Weeches." Quietly, they hurried along the banks of the Saint Lawrence: Cin, Norry, Adam, Stanushka, Mad Matt, Chess, Aria, and the Captain.

In the distance, Aria gawked at the silhouettes of Weeches turned shadow in the first of the morning light. As if fighting the force bearing down on their shoulders, the Weeches slumped beneath Earth's gravity as they pulled the remnants of their shredded bodies toward the river.

Even from there Aria could make out the skin clinging to bone like rags.

"Aria," Cin whispered, pulling Aria's attention from the collective heading their way.

"Why didn't we stay in the boat?" Aria asked.

"Ever seen a horde of Weeches attack a dingy?" Stanushka asked.

"They'll pull the boat apart then pull it under," Angela said.

"And leave you nowhere to run," Cin added.

"Land gives you an out," said Adam. "Last thing you want is to be stuck out in a boat with a pack of Weeches on all sides."

Aria envisioned a horde of Weeches shredding the only source of survival left. A shiver ran up her spine. Picking up pace, she stared at the ground, her thoughts instead turning to the whistle that blew and the rain that stopped too abruptly the night her father vanished. Despite all the crew had done for her, she had her misgivings. If she was to find her father, she would have to venture out alone.

Guilt settled itself into her gut at the thought of abandoning those who had already done so much to help her.

"You won't survive out there alone."

Aria startled at the sound of Norry's voice. He was suddenly beside her walking like an armed guard.

"How?" she asked, staring up at his blonde beard.

"You had the look," he said. "We all have it from time to time. You want to run. Go back to an old home, an old city, an old past."

"Do you let them go?" Aria asked.

"Sure," Norry said. "But they never come back." Norry looked at Aria dead in the eye. "No one ever comes back. No one survives alone long enough to ever make it back."

Norry released Aria from his gaze as his words sank in.

"These few here," Norry said, nodding to the Captain at the front of the line, who had stopped to inspect a wall of forestry. "We are those who didn't go back."

"Didn't you want to?" Aria asked.

"Every day," Norry said.

Aria stared at her feet, unsure of what to say.

"And every day that I don't is a regret," he added.

"Why?"

"Norry!" Angela called from the trees.

Dropping their conversation, Norry clutched the scimitar at his hip and jogged ahead to meet Angela.

"What do you make of this?" Angela said as Norry shifted a branch and peered through the bushes.

"Holy Mary mother of God," Norry muttered. "Fuck damn."

"What is it?" Cin asked.

One by one, the crew made their way to the Captain where each, in turn, gazed through the trees. Aria pulled back a branch and gasped.

An unexpected white light had illuminated the forest, allowing the crew to see miles ahead. And there, before their eyes, a vast saucer, nearly six miles in length, hovered over the Earth. A beam of light poured from its belly onto the forest floor where Weech upon Weech, hundreds at a time, stood. Each Weech, buckling under Earth's gravity, stumbled around for a moment in disorder before settling on a direction. South.

A shadow within the beam caught Aria's eye, and she stared into the light pouring out of the underside of the saucer. Buried within the light, Weeches poured from the ship as if the light itself carefully carried them to land.

"We are so fucked."

"Where are they going?" Norry asked.

"Where indeed?" Angela said, staring at the horde turning south.

"What are we going to do?" Aria asked. "There's no way we can get around this," Chess said.

"It looks like a tomato."

All eyes turned to Matt. He looked sane now more than ever.

"No, it doesn't," Cin argued.

"It does," Matt said. "It looks like a squashed tomato."

"No, it doesn't. It doesn't look anything like a tomato."

"It does," Matt said. "Look. If you tilt your head just right to the left. . . "

Chess and Stani tilted their heads and squinted in an attempt to see.

"I don't see it," Chess said.

Aria stepped away, following the line of trees as she watched the Weeches ride down the beam of light that poured from the saucer's bottom.

"It does too," Matt said, his voice fading further away as Aria walked down the rows of trees, her own thoughts drifting back to the storm, the screaming whistle, and the rain.

"Aria."

A voice Aria knew too well called out from the bushes.

"Dad?" Aria called.

"Aria."

Aria gazed into the forest where the shadows were thick in detail.

"Aria."

Aria stooped to her hands and knees and peered into the shrubs where the voice beckoned her.

"Dad?"

A sickening squelch carried from the foliage and Aria reached forward, pushing back a branch. Growling, a Weech turned up its bloodshot eyes and fixed its gaze on Aria, who was kneeling less than an arm's reach away. Between them, a deer lay sprawled out dead. Its remains dripped from the jaw of the growling Weech, exposing a set of blood-soaked canines.

Aria froze, unable to move, unable to scream.

"Aria," Cin said. "Slowly move away."

Aria didn't move.

"Just pull back, sweetheart. . . "

Shaking, Aria shifted. The Weech lunged, and a flash of scarf and butt flap blocked Aria's vision as Cin pulled Aria back from the carcass.

"Come on!" Mad Matt said, holding the Weech in a headlock. "Be good to the nice lady."

"Matt!" Aria screamed.

"Run!" Matt shouted as he wrapped the scarf around the Weech's face.

"They're coming!" Chess said.

Aria looked to the horizon. The horde of Weeches had abandoned their moving south and were heading toward them.

"Run!" said Matt, wrestling the growling, scarfed Weech.

Weeches pushed through the trees. Norry withdrew his scimitars and slashed the first of the limbs reaching for him.

"Let! Him! Go!" Aria shouted, kicking the Weech's legs.

"My scarf!" Angela shrieked and slid her blades through the chest of a Weech. "Adam! Help him!"

"I'm on it," Adam said, straightening his monocle before shoving a silver rod into a Weech's neck. "Now then everyone." Adam withdrew the stick and raised it to the sky.

"Shield your eyes," he said and pressed an invisible button on the stick, sending a shower of red rain pouring down over the crew and the Weeches.

"Beets?" Aria said. The Weech she was kicking fell dead to the ground and Adam's beet shower drenched it.

Unraveling the scarf from the limp Weech, Matt dove for Adam's silver gadget. "Hey! My screwdriver!" Matt shouted, tripping on the scarf and toppling to the ground.

"Right then. Gotta go," Adam said. "Like. . . now."

The crew lowered their weapons and quickly followed Adam down toward the river as Matt clambered for Adam's gadget.

"Where are we going?" Stani asked.

"There," Adam said, pointing to the other side of the river.

"Wait," Aria said. "You want us to cross the river?"

"Now, please," Adam said. "Before the tincture wears off."

Already the Weeches stirred, rising again to follow them down to the water's edge.

"Faster!" Angela shouted, leading the crew waist-deep into the river.

"Adam! We can't keep going into the river! The current is too strong!"

"We won't go far," Adam replied.

As the crew jumped into the water, the Weeches reached the banks.

"Deeper," Adam said. "Deeper. . . "

The current pushed as they walked further into the river. It reached their waists.

"A little more," Adam said. The crew lined up as the Weeches stepped into the water.

"Form a pyramid," Adam shouted.

"A what?" Cin screamed.

"A pyramid!"

"I'm not standing on anyone's shoulders!" Cin said.

"Not shoulders," Adam shouted back. "A 'V.' Form a 'V!' Angela to the head, Cin! Stani! Behind Angela! Matt, Aria, Chess! Line up! Norry! Stand with me! Now everyone, push against the current. Use each other to break the water tension and strengthen our resistance to the current. And move! Deeper now! Together! We have to move past the current."

As one, the crew pushed through the current as the surface rose to their chests. The Weeches continued to follow through the river.

"Now," Adam said. "Watch."

The moment the first Weech stepped into the current, the water ripped him apart and shoved his feet out from under him. More followed, each Weech proceeding through the river on their own. The crew watched as each Weech was ripped to shreds by the current and pushed downstream.

"Adam!" Chess called. "We can't do this forever!"

"No, we can't!" Adam said.

"When I say jump," Matt shouted.

"No!" Aria, Adam, and Norry cried.

"Do you have a better idea?"

The crew looked among themselves, each waiting for the other to form a plan.

"Alright then!" Matt said. "When I say jump. . . jump!"

The crew jumped and the current pushed them down the river and away from the landing site. The Weeches proceeded to follow, but the current too quickly pushed the crew away.

"Ada—" Angela swallowed a mouthful of water.

As the current tossed and turned the crew, Adam battled the water's course and reached for his boot. From within his boot, he withdrew a long silver tube. The water pulled him under and Adam forced his head to the surface, aimed, and fired a claw-like hand toward the banks.

"A Dale—" The water pulled Matt under the surface.

"Hold o—" Adam's head went under. He resurfaced. "Hold on!"

Angela grabbed Adam's arm and reached for Norry, who grabbed a hold. Aria and Matt came next as Chess grabbed Norry's belt. Cin grabbed Chess's hand, then took hold of Angela's hand. Angela reached and took hold of Stani, who was most concerned about keeping her bazooka above the water's surface.

Pressing a button, Adam's line fed by the silver tube churned, reeling the crew in on the line.

"I'm a fish! I'm a fish!" Matt squawked, delighted by the human chain they had formed in the water.

One by one, they reached the bank and pulled themselves ashore. In turn, they plopped to the grass, gasping to catch their breath as they rested there.

"Remind me," Chess said. "To punch Matt when I have the strength to move."

"Hey, Captain," Norry said from the ground. "How about we call it a night?"

"Yeah," Angela said, between breaths. "Let's do that."

"Is this even safe?" Aria asked.

Safe.

Silence stretched over the crew.

"Safe," Matt mused. "Is anywhere safe anymore?"

"Come on then," Norry said, pulling himself to his feet. "Let's build a fire. Check supplies. Build a shelter. Come on, Garlic Man. We can cut down some of these larger pine branches to form a lean-to for the night."

"Right-o," Matt said.

"I'll scout the area," Chess said, rising to her feet.

"I'm going hunting," Cin said. "I'll see if I can find some wildlife in the area we can snare."

"Hold on, Cin," Stani said. "I'm coming with you."

The crew dispersed as Angela and Adam began counting supplies.

"Alright," Angela said. "What do we have with us? What did we lose?"

Hugging her arms tight to her chest, Aria slipped into the forest unseen.

# Chapter Ten

Aria wandered into the trees, stopping now and then to pick up a random stick.

She settled on a thin birch tree that had fallen. A bit of pressure in the right place would be enough to break it into sizable pieces. She hoisted an end of the birch and positioned it onto its own stump as the last several hours ran through her mind. Aria dropped her foot down on the log, but it only bounced in response.

Aria kicked again. The log bounced. Again and again, Aria kicked as images of her father and Caius raced through her head. Aria kicked. The Weeches closing in. . .

Kick.

*Caius.*

Kick.

*The spaceship.*

Kick.

*The Weeches.*

Kick.

*Her father.*

Aria fell to the ground and sobbed, shuddering at the chill in the air, angry with her own limitations.

"Aria."

Aria gasped and gazed at Mad Matt, standing in just his loincloth, boots, and the scarf.

"What do you want?" Aria said, sniffling as she shoved the tears away.

"No need to hide the tears, love. You're right to have them."

"Yeah, and what do you know about it? About any of it?"

"You've lost someone close to you. That much is apparent."

Aria hugged her knees to her chest. "I shouldn't be here."

"No," Matt said. "You shouldn't. None of us should."

"I just want my father back. Instead, I'm here with... I don't even know what this is! It's madness! That's what this is!"

Matt settled on the ground beside Aria and sighed.

"Bristol," he said.

"What?"

"I'm from Bristol."

Aria studied Matt's face as he recalled a life long since lost.

"I was on my way home from work when the invasions in England started. The prime minister was the first to go, and our cabinets. The royal family. I wasn't feeling well that day, so I left. I don't think I had ever been so happy to have a stomach bug. If I had stayed... If I was feeling well, I never would have left early and missed the slaughter. I would have died right alongside my co-workers."

Aria gazed, too stunned to answer.

"They took out the media first. I learned that later. They realized an attack would be best if the public remained ignorant. No one saw it coming. No one knew... We all were sitting ducks."

"If the media was taken out, then how did you know? About the prime minister and the governments and the royal family?"

"Because, love," Matt said, "I was working with the prime minister to arrange the formal meeting of Weech to human. I rolled out the bloody welcome mat for them. Every media source, every government body was organized in the same building when they launched their attack. Everyone able to communicate and rule, wiped out in a single move. No one saw it coming. No one was prepared or even aware of the attacks that would follow. No TV, no radio, no newspaper, no satellite. . . no internet or phones. . . All of it gone. Our only sources of communication were word of mouth. Not very effective when reporting on a full-scale invasion."

"Everything gone," Aria said.

"Yep." Matt nodded. "Just caught me a Lapris, too."

Aria looked at Matt in all seriousness. Together they burst into a fit of laughter. After a moment, they settled down.

"You were captured by Caius?" Aria asked.

Matt nodded. "I was."

"Why? What did he want?"

"Can't tell you that, love. Can't give Caius any more reason to hunt you down."

Aria looked to the skies, and Matt rose to his feet.

"Matt?"

"Yes, love?"

"Do you think my father is alive?"

"If he's anything at all like you, he is."

Aria watched as Matt headed back to the camp, sitting for a while longer as she stared up at the sky.

"Just beautiful," she said.

Standing, she brushed the leaf litter from her backside and repositioned her foot onto the weakest part of the log. Finding her balance, she bounced lightly, ready to shift all her weight onto the log when a cold hand clamped down on her mouth, twisting her arm around and into her back, and holding her head back into a hard, cold chest.

"My clan is positioned and ready," breathed Caius. "You move. You fight. They kill."

Caius added a soft kiss to Aria's ear.

"Come," Caius said. "Someone has requested a meeting with you."

Caius opened his mouth and sank his canines into the flesh of Aria's neck. She felt herself fall limp into Caius's arms and all the world went black.

# Chapter Eleven

"**A**ria!" Norry called across the field.

"Aria!" Cin shouted.

"Anything?" Angela asked.

"Nothing," said Adam.

"Captain," Norry said, "we can't keep doing this. It's a miracle we haven't attracted the Weeches already."

"We have," said Chess, panting as she joined the group. "Stani and I've been holding them off."

"Has anyone found anything?" Angela asked.

Stanushka joined them. Fresh Weech blood covered her arms and her barrels were smoking. "We can't stay out here in the open," she said.

"She's right," Adam said. "We need to find cover. Fall back. Regroup. Assess. Execute."

"I'll not leave her," Norry said.

"We're not leaving her," Cin said.

"Adam's right," Angela said. "We can't help Aria if we don't first take care of ourselves."

"Fall back to where?" Norry said. "The Slush Brain is gone. We have no home. No supplies. No Aria. . . "

"Singer Castle."

All eyes turned to Matt, who had remained eerily quiet since Aria's disappearance.

"Matt," Angela said. "What do you know?"

"Weeches don't abduct," Matt said. "If the Weeches had found her, there would be pieces of her everywhere."

The words struck the crew, leaving a sickening silence among them. "If she were here," Matt continued. "She'd answer. She isn't here, which means. . . "

"Caius," Angela said.

"Caius," Matt confirmed.

"We have no ship," Cin said.

"No provisions," Adam said.

"And no plan," said Stani.

"And you want us to launch an attack on Singer Castle?" Chess asked.

"It can't be done," said Norry.

"It can," Matt said. "Besides, you haven't considered our greatest asset."

"What?" Cin said.

"Me," Matt said. "You forget—" Matt gave Angela's 15-foot scarf a flourish, wrapping an end around his neck once, twice, then thrice. "I'm the Doctor."

The crew watched in a daze as Mad Matt—wearing nothing but boots, a garlic-infused loincloth and a *Doctor Who* scarf—proudly strode toward the river with half the scarf trailing behind him.

"Are we really following a near naked Englishman into battle?"

"Yes," Adam said. "Yes, I think we are."

"But he doesn't even have laces in his boots," Cin said.

"No," Angela said. "No, he doesn't."

"Angela," Chess loudly whispered. "He thinks he's the Doctor."

Angela's mouth tightened. "Yes. Yes, he does."

"Do you think we should tell him that he's not?" Adam asked.

"I don't think that would matter," said Angela.

"We're going to die," Norry said. "Aren't we?"

"Yes," Angela said. "Yes, we are." Shaking her head, Angela followed Matt toward the river, leading her crew to Singer Castle.

# Chapter Twelve

The haze broke and the sleep faded as Aria awakened in the dark to the sounds of sobs, screams, and the familiar gurgle of Weech speech. A lingering stale stench of damp basement and human filth clung to the air. Fire seared Aria's shoulders, stretched by chains that forced her arms painfully wide.

Screams wafted from somewhere in the distance, fueling her panic. Aria pulled at the chains. She braced her foot behind her on the wall and pulled again at the chains that dug into her wrists.

"I wouldn't move too much," a smooth drawl carried across the cell.

Aria froze and peered through the darkness to the end of the room where a burst of light illuminated Caius's tall silhouette.

With the light, Aria could see a pair of Weeches chained close enough to devour her should she manage to escape. Behind her, horror engulfed her at the site of cages and cells all lining the wall like a corridor and each crammed to the hilt with the last of the humans.

Women mostly cried silently and held their children close to them in the filth.

"What the fuck are you doing to them?" Aria said.

Caius turned to the cages behind him.

"We've saved them."

"This is madness!"

"This is our only chance of survival," Caius said.

"Then you have no business surviving!"

"Are we any different than humans who raise the cattle to eat?"

"We don't sleep with cattle! We don't wed them and breed with them!" Aria said.

"Your myths would beg to differ."

"You're monsters!"

"We have a right to survive," Caius said.

"Not when your survival is at our expense! You're no better than the Weeches!"

"The Weeches won't give you a chance to live. They'll rip you apart."

"No different than what you've done here!" Aria said.

"The Weeches aren't humane about it."

"And this! This is what you call humane!? Oh, what difference does it all make! We're arguing over which of you two monsters is the worst. And you want me to be part of it!?"

"You are a part of this, Aria. You were born into this, decades ago."

"I was never any such thing," Aria said.

Caius turned to better look upon the humans cowering in their cages.

"These are all that's left, too small or sick or young to eat, so we store them down here until we have use for them."

"They're people!"

"They're lab rats," Caius corrected.

The horror of the situation sunk in. As if to say, 'let me show you,' Caius stepped back, aiming the light to shine down a corridor where tables, instruments, corpses, and the source of the distant screams resided.

Aria thrashed as she kicked against the wall, paying no mind to the cuts and the blood as the metal cut into her wrists or the Weeches excited by her sudden burst of movement.

Exhausted, she slumped to the floor as much as the chains would let her and cried.

"What the hell are you?" Aria said.

"Exactly what you made us," Caius said. "Forced to live in secret in holes underground. Forced to live like animals coiled away in dens to escape the genocide of Men. Everything we are today, you made... evolved to adapt to the lifestyle gifted by humans. Venom that paralyzes our prey, strength and speed that surpasses our predators... "

"And the bloodlust and cannibalism?"

Caius smiled. "Oh, no, sweet Aria... That is a choice. Or, it was once." Caius withdrew a vial and held it so Aria could see it in the light.

"What is that?" Aria asked.

"This." Caius admired the vial like a lover. "This is a virus, manufactured, developed, and perfected within these dungeons. The infected will go on living with the craving of bloodlust. It affects the brain and withdraws all inhibitions. It builds artificial muscle and sharpens illusion."

"So, it's a vial of booze," Aria said.

Caius chuckled.

"There are side effects."

"What kind of side effects?" Aria asked.

"Babbling. Insane ramblings. Sometimes delusions that the host is someone they're not, or they contain superpowers that aren't there."

At once, Aria's thoughts turned to Mad Matt.

"In the average host, it can have a number of effects." Caius shifted his loving gaze to Aria. "But in the right host, it does something completely different."

"Like what?" Aria asked. Her heart slammed into her chest.

"We found a way to alter the chemical components of a host. . . make them what they aren't. Transform them."

Arias scoffed. "But that's technology that's way beyond our science. We can't possible come close to that kind of science."

"Not us, perhaps," Caius said. "But they aren't." Caius raised a brow in the direction of the Weech clawing at Aria.

She gasped. "No!"

"The same venom used in the Weeches to assimilate human to Weech is the same venom contained in this vial. We've found a way to assimilate humans and make them into whatever we want. . . and you, Aria, are the first."

"No!" Aria screamed and thrashed against the wall.

"Your DNA makeup is unique. Only your blood will serve as the host we are looking for. DNA passed on from your parentage."

Aria froze. "My father. . . "

"I was there, you know," Caius said. "That night when your father vanished."

Aria's eyes widened with attention.

"The rains were pouring. . . and the siren blared. . . You never wondered why I knew to be there? How I came to be there that night?"

"Where is my father?" Aria whispered. "Did you. . . " Fire burned the tip of her nose. "Where is he?" she asked, fighting her chains again. "What did you do to him? Where did you take him? Is he here?"

Slowly, Caius walked to Aria.

"Where. . ." Exhausted, Aria fell back against the wall. "Where is my father?"

Caius pulled back a lock of Aria's hair.

"Please," Aria said. A single tear slid down her nose.

"I understand your disdain for me," Caius said. Gently, he cupped her cheek in his hand, allowing her head to rest in his palm. "I could give you anything," he said. "You would want for nothing."

"I would sooner die than live a moment of my life with you," Aria hissed.

Caius frowned and withdrew a syringe from his coat. Swiftly, he fitted the vial into the syringe.

"I have all of eternity to wait," Caius said. "You will learn to love me before this life is through."

A fresh bout of screaming forced their attention to the rooms above them.

"But. . . seeing as I don't have an eternity. . ." Caius dove and plunging his teeth into one side of Aria's neck, he shoved the needle into the other. Aria screamed as Caius emptied the vial. A moment later, she fell silent against the wall.

# Chapter Thirteen

Caius fled up the main stairs. His coolness and dignity vanished with his rage as he stomped toward the main hall.

"We're under attack," a vampire said as he met Caius on the steps.

"I have no tolerance for this," Caius said. "Who is it?"

"The pirates are here."

Caius froze and released a sigh. "Is he with them?"

"He is."

Caius continued up the stairs as before. "Don't let them leave. Dead or alive, the others can stay, but that Englishman does not leave here again. His cells contain all our work over the last twenty years."

* * *

Back in the dungeons where Aria lay, the pair of chained Weeches snarled and pulled against their bonds. A woman dressed in clothes tattered by filth and time effortlessly stepped forward, raising the blade in her hand. The katana slid through the Weech's head and it fell to the floor dead. As she turned, she swung the blade with her, cutting through the neck of the second Weech, which fell to the dungeon floor.

The woman kneeled beside Aria, who had begun shaking as if with fever. Upon closer inspection, she could see that Aria's skin had already paled in the likeness of Caius. The woman withdrew a vial from her rags and quickly pulled the liquid into a syringe. Carefully, she injected the fluid into Aria.

"Shh," she cooed and gently stroked Aria's face. "You're alright now."

The shaking subsided as a calm settled over Aria and the color returned to her cheeks. A moment later, the woman was unlocking Aria's chains.

# Chapter Fourteen

Screams filled the Hall.

"What is it?" one of the vampires called.

"Where is Caius?"

More screams followed a distant explosion. The castle rattled under the tremor.

Kylie left the room, descending the grand stairs as a vampire flew to the window, desperate to look out across the grounds of Singer Island.

"What's happen—"

A blast threw the door into hall, sending an avalanche of rock, dust, debris, and splinters of wood with it.

'*Whoa! Come with me now!*' blared as the cloud of dust cleared. The Slush Brain crew emerged with a lingering stench of beets. Mad Matt dressed in his boots, *Doctor Who* scarf, and loincloth armed with a bucket of water balloons, Cin Dixon with her flask and swords, Adam equipped with a cup of black tea that he slowly sipped with a world of patience, Stanushka, with a set of smoking M32 grenade launchers poised at each arm, Chess sporting her flintlock, and Norry, armed at the ready with a pair of scimitars. At the center of the crew Angela stood, a tiara just visible under the captain's hat and a katana in her hand.

Norry paused the boom box.

"A boom box?" Cin asked, wrinkling her face at Norry. "Seriously? How old are you?"

"Caius!" Angela shouted. "Come on out! El Capitan wants to play!"

"Kylie," Norry growled across the room. "Where is he?"

Kylie stared from the stairs with a bored expression.

"Oh, the rabble has arrived."

"We want Aria," Matt announced.

Caius smiled and a tall blond vampire appeared from behind the stairs.

"Aria," Caius said. "That's a tall order. . . and it will cost you."

"We're not here to negotiate," Angela said.

Another vampire appeared from the hole in the wall behind the Slush Brain crew.

"We're here to cash in," said Stani.

"You have some nerve breaking down my door. . . " Caius said.

"Wall," Chess corrected.

"To be fair, the door is somewhere around here," Norry said.

A third and fourth vampire joined the ranks as Caius riled the crew.

"I'll make you this offer," he said. "Leave now without that man, and I'll forget how stupid you were blasting down my door."

"Wall," Adam corrected.

"Matt is one of us," Angela declared.

"When did that happen?" Cin asked, peering at the half-naked Englishman still reeking of garlic.

"He stays with us," Angela said.

Caius's nostrils visibly flared at the crew's defiance.

"Caius," Kylie droned from the stairs.

"Not now, Kylie," he said.

"Caius," Kylie said again.

Caius looked at Kylie. "Not now, Kylie!"

Beet juice splattered Caius's chest. The remnants of a red water balloon hung to his vest. All attention turned to Mad Matt, who stood, armed at the ready with a second water balloon.

"Get them," Caius said and the vampires leapt into action, meeting Stani's guns head-on.

As Chess unloaded her flintlocks, Norry stepped in, dual-wielding his scimitars and taking heads faster than they could jump in to meet his blades.

"Now," Adam said. On cue, Matt launched a barrage of beet balloons. Beet juice splattered everywhere, mingling with the blood and the booze as Cin traded off her flask for a dagger that carved a path through the teeth.

Side by side, Angela, Adam, and Cin marched past the fight to the steps.

"This way," Angela said. "Matt said she'd be near the lowest floor—"

Angela froze.

"What's wrong?" Cin asked as Adam pushed past Angela.

"My god. . . " Adam said. "Aria."

At a doorway descending a flight of stairs stood a woman with the last bit of strength, holding Aria in her arms.

She collapsed and Adam dove, catching Aria and the woman before she hit the floor. Angela and Cin fell to his side and gently helped Aria and the woman down.

"Aria's okay," Adam said. "Looks like she's just passed out."

"P-Plea. . . " the woman sputtered.

"Shh," Angela hushed as Cin pulled back the woman's rags.

"Who is she?" Angela asked.

"She's Aria's mother."

Cin, Adam, and Angela turned to the voice behind them and gazed at Kylie.

Adam, Angela, and Cin exchanged looks and stared at the woman dressed in blood and rags. Beneath the filth, they could just make out the resemblance.

"It looks like she's lost a lot of blood," Cin said, pulling back the last layer. Under a shaking hand caked in blood, she found the woman's wound: a gaping hole below a shattered rib.

"It looks like she took down a few of our own on her way up," Kylie said.

Aria's mother shifted the blade that lay forgotten on the floor.

"G-gi. . . ve. . . " she whispered.

Angela accepted the blade. "We will. . . We'll make sure Aria gets it."

The woman gasped as if relieved and attempted a smile through the pain as she took in her last few breaths. A moment later, she exhaled and the life left her.

"Come on," Adam said. "We can't stay here."

Adam scooped Aria off the floor and stopped. A horde of Weeches had found their way onto the island and were making their way toward the gaping hole in the wall.

"Well?" Adam said. "Let's move on then."

Without question, Angela followed closely behind.

"But. . . " Cin stared, dumbfounded at the number of Weeches approaching the wall.

"No worries," Adam said, leading the way calmly over debris.

"Slush Brain! Let's go!" Angela announced, paying the battle no mind.

Stani had continued to unleash round upon round on the vampires jumping overhead beside Chess as Matt proceeded to launch beet balloons at Caius, who was locked in battle against Norry.

From the corner of her eye, Angela saw it: Caius stole a glance at Aria asleep in Adam's arms. A final blow, knocking Norry off balance, and he jumped.

Adam froze as Angela leapt out in front to take the blow for Aria, and instead, greeted silence. Between Caius and Aria, Chess stood unmoving and suspended at the end of Caius's arm.

Chess coughed, spitting blood.

Caius withdrew his hand from Chess's chest. She was dead before she hit the ground.

An ear-splitting scream filled the castle as Stani charged. Angela swung her sword at Caius, who dodged the attack. Forgetting the bucket of beet balloons, Matt ran into the fight.

"No," Norry said, grabbing Matt before he could get too close. "We need to leave," Norry said. "Adam!"

"Got it," Adam said. "Everyone! Exit right."

Norry pulled Matt toward the door as Angela and Cin met Stani head-on, joining Adam as they started toward the door.

Caius lunged and slammed hard into Kylie, who held him in place.

"Kylie!" Caius growled. "Release me!"

Angela looked back.

"Get out of here, Slush Brain!" Kylie said.

"You've chosen your side, sister!" said Caius.

The Slush Brain crew clambered back through the hole in the wall where Adam passed Aria to Norry.

"Caius," Kylie said. "Go to hell."

From his vest pocket, Adam withdrew a pocketwatch and gave a tug to the hem of his vest to straighten it. As if casually checking the time, he straightened his monocle and opened the watch. Every bit of beet juice ignited, engulfing the hall in flames.

# Epilogue

Angela stared into the distance, where a saucer was beaming down Weech after Weech upon the soil of Alexandria Bay. Behind her, Singer Castle burned. Cin and Norry vanished below deck with Aria eager to get her settled down somewhere comfortable. Adam set to work right away adjusting Stani's guns.

Somewhere in the night, the Professor was lost to the world. Chess's remains were lost to the flames. It was too soon to feel the hurt and loss. By morning, the battle fatigue would have turned into shellshock. Maybe in a day or two, they would feel enough again to grieve for Chess. For now, the need to survive was too prominent.

"Captain?"

Angela turned to Mad Matt, still standing there in nothing but boots, a garlic-soaked loincloth, and her 15-foot scarf.

"What do we do now?" he asked.

Exhausted, Angela looked out to the Weech ship and the only feasible solution left.

"To the Weeches."

* * *

*Congratulations! You have boarded the HMS Slush Brain! Each of my books come with buried treasure, a free bookmark (I can only ship to the US), and "behind the scenes" material.*

*You can find all of this and more at*
http://angelabchrysler.com/
?page_id=16418&preview=true
Enter the case-sensitive password "Batman Sucks!" to access the Slush Brain bootie!

*The story continues in Zombies from Space... Fists in the Dark!*
*Read free at* http://www.angelabchrysler.com/
**Free Bookmark**
Claim your free Zombies from Space... and Vampires bookmark at
http://angelabchrysler.com/secret-page/

Dear reader,

We hope you enjoyed reading *Zombies from Space and Vampires*. Please take a moment to leave a review, even if it's a short one. Your opinion is important to us.

Discover more books by Angela B. Chrysler at https://www.nextchapter.pub/authors/angela-b-chrysler

Want to know when one of our books is free or discounted? Join the newsletter at http://eepurl.com/bqqB3H

Best regards,
Angela B. Chrysler and the Next Chapter Team

# About the Author

*Angela B. Chrysler is a writer, logician, philosopher, and die-hard nerd who studies theology, historical linguistics, music composition, and medieval European history in New York with a dry sense of humor and an unusual sense of sarcasm. She lives in a garden with her family and cats.*

http://www.angelabchrysler.com/

https://www.goodreads.com/user/show/36016085-angela-chrysler

https://twitter.com/abchryslerabc

https://www.facebook.com/pages/Angela-B-Chrysler/755206654548539

# More Books

More books by Angela B. Chrysler

**Dolor and Shadow (Tales of the Drui Book #1)**

*As the elven city burns, Princess Kallan is taken to Alfheim while a great power begins to awaken within her. Desperate to keep the child hidden, her abilities are suppressed and her memory erased. But the gods have powers as well, and it is only a matter of time before they find the child again.*

When Kallan, the elven witch, Queen of Lorlenalin, fails to save her dying father, she inherits her father's war and vows revenge on the one man she believes is responsible: Rune, King of Gunir. But nothing is as it seems, and the gods are relentless. A twist of fate puts Kallan into the protection of the man she has sworn to kill, and Rune into possession of power he does not understand.

From Alfheim, to Jotunheim, and then lost in the world of Men, these two must form an alliance to make their way home, and try to solve the lies of the past and of the Shadow that hunts them all.

**Fire and Lies (Tales of the Drui Book #2)**

Blood waters the fields of Alfheim. War rips across the land of usurped kings and elves. The Fae gods draw near, and Queen Kallan's strength is tested as she follows King Rune into Alfheim. But the Shadow Beast caged within Rune's body writhes in hunger, and Kallan's newest companion, Bergen the legendary Berserk, is determined to end the conflict with her life.

As the witch, the king, and the berserk come together, the truth buried within the past resurfaces. Now, Kallan must master a dormant power or watch her kingdom fall to the Fae who will stop at nothing to keep their lies.

Fire and Lies (Tales of the Drui Book #2) picks up right where Dolor and Shadow left off, concluding one chapter of Kallan's life as the next chapter begins.

**Broken**

*And Death it calls as the stone crow breaks. Streaks of blood malform its face.*

*Death becomes its withered eyes and the shadows whisper, "Lies."*

When William, a young journalist, seeks out Elizabeth, an acclaimed author, in hopes to write her biography, the recluse grants him twenty-four hours to hear her story. What unfolds are a wide range of traumas that teeter on the edge of macabre and psychological thriller.

While toggling the lines of insanity, Elizabeth examines her neglect, rape, abuse, torture, and pedophilia-filled past. The more Elizabeth delves into her psyche, the more William witnesses the multiple mental conditions Elizabeth developed to cope with a life without love, comfort, protection, trust, physical human contact, affection, therapy, or medication.

*With the use of existentialism, I wrote Broken in an attempt to philosophical determine what I had become and why. Instead, I found the awareness I needed to seek help. Broken is the road map I took to arrive at "Awareness."*

Zombies from Space and Vampires
ISBN: 978-4-86750-852-7

Published by
Next Chapter
1-60-20 Minami-Otsuka
170-0005 Toshima-Ku, Tokyo
+818035793528
22nd June 2021

www.ingramcontent.com/pod-product-compliance
Lightning Source LLC
LaVergne TN
LVHW041457190726
843491LV00008B/2401

* 9 7 8 4 8 6 7 5 0 8 5 2 7 *